W9-AUI-851

Sheep in Wolves' Clothing

FOR MY MOTHER & FATHER

SPECIAL THANKS TO
ALISON SAGE

Copyright © 1995 by Satoshi Kitamura
All rights reserved
First published in Great Britain by Andersen Press Ltd., 1995
Color separations by Photolitho AG
Printed in Mexico
First American edition, 1996

Library of Congress Cataloging-in-Publication Data
Kitamura, Satoshi.
Sheep in wolves' clothing / Satoshi Kitamura. — 1st American ed.
p. cm.
[1. Sheep—Fiction. 2. Wolves—Fiction. 3. Mystery and detective stories.] I. Title.
PZ7.K6713Sh 1996 [E]—dc20 95-18199 CIP AC

Sheep in Wolves' Clothing

SATOSHI KITAMURA

FARRAR, STRAUS AND GIROUX
NEW YORK

One morning in late summer
Hubert was having breakfast when Georgina came jumping over the fence.
"Good morning, Hubert," she said. "I'm going to the beach
for the last swim of the year. Want to come?"
"Why not?" said Hubert.

As they trotted down the hill, they heard the honk of a horn.
It was Gogol in his brand-new convertible.
"Where are you off to?" he called.
"We're going to the beach for a swim," said Hubert.
"Hop in! I'll take you," said Gogol. He made the engine roar.
"Hold tight!"

They sped along the country lane.
"I love the feel of the wind fluffing my wool," said Georgina.

Suddenly the car made a clanking noise and started to lose speed. "Something's wrong," said Gogol. He checked the engine, pulling this and flicking that. "It can't be serious, because the car's so new—but these expensive cars are very difficult to fix."

YOU MEAN YOU CAN'T FIX IT YOURSELF.

IN OTHER WORDS, NO.

The three sheep sat around the car.
What could they do?
"What's the matter?" called a voice.
They looked over and saw a boat
coming toward them.
It was Captain Bleat.
Hubert told the Captain about
their trip to the beach.

"I'm going to the sea myself," said the Captain. "Why don't you join me? You can find a mechanic later to fix your car." The offer was perfect, so they went aboard. The boat drifted along the river and Hubert lay on the deck looking up at the blue sky.

When the boat reached the sea, the three sheep thanked the Captain
and raced to the beach.

They did exercises first and were just about to run into the sea when...

"Hey! Wait!" called a voice.
Four wolves were playing miniature golf on the sand.
"I don't want to be rude," said one of them,
"but think of your beautiful coats! The salt water will ruin them."
"I guess you're right," said Gogol.
"Look," the wolf went on, "we can watch your coats.
Why don't you pile them up under our sunshade?"
"Sounds like a good idea," said Hubert.

"Have a nice swim," called the wolves.

After swimming and splashing for an hour or so, the three sheep returned to the beach tired and happy.

OH, THAT WAS GREAT!

MY BREAST STROKE'S GETTING BETTER!

I'M FREEZING!

They searched everywhere, but there was not a single wisp of wool to be seen.

There were tire tracks in the sand.
"Let's follow these tracks," said Gogol. "They might lead us to the wolves."

They walked all afternoon until finally they reached the town.

"I'm hungry, but my money was in my coat pocket!" grumbled Gogol.
It was getting dark and the three sheep were exhausted.

The sheep
sat by a fountain
in the middle
of the town square.
"Of course," said Georgina at last,
"there is one sheep we could turn to."
"Who's that?" said Hubert.
"My cousin Elliott. He's a detective."
Georgina led the others to her cousin's office.
The glass window said: ELLIOTT BAA - PRIVATE DETECTIVE.

**When the sheep had finished their story, the detective was silent for a long time.
"There are quite a few wolves in town," he said at last.
"Most of them are up to no good and play golf."**

Elliott put on his glasses and stood up. "I need some fresh air," he said, and walked out of his office.

It was past midnight and not many creatures were about. Suddenly the detective paused. He was staring at something.

"It's only a gang of cats playing rugby," said Gogol.
"Look how they're playing," said Elliott. "All tangled up."
"That's how rugby is always played," whispered Georgina.
"But look at the ball," said the detective.
"It's getting smaller and smaller."
Soon the cats were all tied up.

"Kids." Elliott spoke to the cats. "Tell us where you found
your ball and we'll help you out of this mess."

The cats told the sheep that they had found the ball of wool in the road.
"So it stretched all the way?" said the detective. "Good.
Come and give us a hand if you like games."
Elliott began following the wool along the road.

The wool stretched along the pavement
and around lampposts. It wound around corners
and ran across gutters, until at last they found it caught
under the door of a seedy building.

Elliott whispered to them and
the cats purred with excitement.
Softly, they opened the door.
At the top of the stairs was a sign:

WOLFGANG & BROS.
QUALITY KNITWEAR

They could hear laughter and the muffled sound of jazz on the radio. The detective knocked. The voices stopped. Slowly, the door opened, and a wolf peered out. Elliott pushed past him into the room.

"We've come for our coats," said the detective.
The wolves' jaws dropped, and their knitting needles froze.
But soon they got over their shock.
"Whoever heard of a sheep picking a fight
with wolves?" snarled one.
"Let's get him, boys!"

The wolves sprang to their feet.
Elliott grabbed a basketful of wool
and threw it into the air.
"At 'em, cats!" he shouted.

Balls of wool flew in all directions as the cats jumped into the room.

The sheep joined in.

It wasn't like their game of rugby but the cats thought it was more fun. The wolves did not like it at all.

"Game over!"
shouted Gogol triumphantly.
"You won't get your coats back," said the wolves.
"We've unraveled them."
"Then we'll take these instead," said Hubert, picking up a large bag.

When the sheep and cats came out onto the street, it was almost daybreak.
Gogol thanked the cats for their help.
"Not at all," said the cats. "We had a great time."

"I'll give you a lift home," offered Elliott.
"Thanks," said Georgina. "You know, Elliott,
you are a brilliant detective."
"I'm sorry I was too late to save your coats," said Elliott.
"It wasn't your fault," said Georgina.
"And these will do for now,"
said Hubert, who was still carrying the large bag.

"I'm starving," said Gogol.
"Me too, I need breakfast," said Hubert.
"Let's go back to the meadow,"
said Georgina.

NOV 25.94

And that is what they did.

DATE DUE		
NOV 1 5 2004		
DEC 2 2 2004		
MAY 1 6 2005		